When A Lark Sings

A Short Story

Grace Pakes

D1527736

For Mr. Dobner

Thanks for all your support, I'm glad you liked it.

When A Lark Sings

Part One

Lark and Theo. Everyone in town, no matter how disclosed from society they were, knew the names and the ways of the young teenagers who possessed them. From their kind and innocent smiles to the sounds of the bells on their bikes ringing continuously as they rode down each and every street in town, laughing the whole way. Laughing about nothing in particular, per se. Sometimes they laughed about a poem Lark had just made up off the top of her head; other times it would be about some rude remark Theo had just made about the mindless sycophant that made their school lives miserable. What it was they were laughing about never really mattered, though, because they would always laugh, despite everything else. They would always laugh because they were always happy. And they were always happy because they were always together.

Saying these two were best friends would be an understatement because they weren't *just* each other's best friends, they were each other's lifelines. Every minute they could spend with each other they would. They were constantly talking to each other, no matter how long it had been since they had last seen each other. I know people like these are talked about a lot in books and movies. Two people that are inseparable. Two people who never get a moment alone off of pure choice. But then you go out into the real world, and you don't really see these people. Maybe in middle or elementary school, but everyone else past that age seems more independent. But trust me, I know from experience, these people do in fact exist.

As I can recall, there was only one summer in their entire friendship that they didn't spend together. However, that one summer was enough time to change everything between them. Three months where Lark left town with no explanation of her destination, leaving Theo alone and vulnerable to the rest of the world. Three months that I can't really tell you about, because although it altered their entire relationship, not much actually happened during them. But what I can tell you about, though, is what happened before and after that summer.

Some time ago, not long before they were to finish their Sophomore year, Lark and Theo sat on his porch, playing Texas Hold'em and listening to All Time Low while arguing over who was the best character on *Friends*.

"I don't care what you say, Lark, it's Chandler. I mean, could it *be* more obvious?" Theo said, mocking the character he admired so.

"As if, it's definitely Phoebe. No doubt about it," she remarked, showing off her full house while Theo threw his hand down in frustration, exposing that he only had two pairs.

"You're both wrong, it's Joey." Theo's mom said, butting into their conversation, but making up for it by handing them both a bottle of Sun Drop.

"No way," they said simultaneously, causing the three of them to stifle small laughs.

As Theo's mom went back inside and Lark sipped on her soda, she turned to Theo and said, "I got a new one for you."

He knew exactly what she had meant when she said this. Lark often wrote poems for Theo, most of which had no meaning at all, but they meant a lot to him.

"Let's hear it, then," he replied.

She cleared her throat before dramatically staring at him with her hand out in a Shakespearean manner and reciting,

"*Poor young Theodore Gray,*

Sat on his porch, his mind astray

For he thought and he thought

And deny he could not

The best Friends character was Phoebe Buffay."

Every poem she ever wrote him always started with "*Poor young Theodore Gray*". This was strange to most considering

Gray wasn't Theo's surname, but it made sense to them because it was the surname he wished he carried. Ever since eighth grade when they had to read it, Theo had wanted to be just like the title character from *The Picture of Dorian Gray*. He admired how suave and confident he was, and envied him. All he wanted to be was the handsome young Victorian man who was good enough to be the topic of Oscar Wilde's only novel. Except, you know, without all the sex-craze, blood lust, ruthlessness and insanity.

"Deny he could not?" he questioned.

"I'll admit, that was a bit of a stretch, but I'm still proud of it," she answered.

"Yeah. I still liked it, even though you're wrong." He chortled before continuing to ask, "Are you staying for dinner?"

"I probably shouldn't," she sighed, "I've got to get home to Mamó."

He nodded and picked up the cards, slowly stuffing them back into the box as she finished off her soda.

"Tell your mom thanks, I'll call you when I get home." she smiled, then she was gone.

Lark's home life was interesting. Not bad, but interesting. She'd never known a single thing about her father. Whether he was dead or alive, if he'd left them by choice or force, his name, what he looked like, nothing. But she did know her mother. She was the most hard-working person Lark had ever known. She worked so hard to give Lark a good life, but she still made time for her. It was like she was an angel sent from above. Lark's grandmother used to call her mom "bronntanas Dia" which means "gift of God" in Gaelic.

Sadly, three years ago Lark's mom passed away from stage four leukemia. Ever since then she'd been living with her Irish-immigrant grandmother (mamó). It's not often you meet someone who only speaks Gaelic, but in her mamó's case, it was true. She tried to learn English, but it was a lost cause. She couldn't pronounce the words correctly no matter how hard she tried. So instead, Lark learned Gaelic and had been speaking in it fluently ever since she was nine.

As Lark stepped through the front door, she immediately saw mamó asleep on the couch, *The Price is Right* playing on the TV. She tried to be extra quiet while going to her room, but being the clumsy young girl that she was, she tripped twice up the stairs, making loud thuds each time. Thankfully, mamó was a very heavy sleeper and was unaffected by the noise. When she got to her room she closed the door quickly and snatched her phone out of her pocket, immediately FaceTiming Theo.

"Miss me already? You're so needy," he said as the call connected.

"Stop acting like you wouldn't have done the same thing if the roles were reversed," she responded, rolling her eyes.

"I wouldn't have. *I'm* not needy."

"Sure you aren't." She laughed remembering all the times he had texted her as soon as she'd walked out of his room.

"So," Theo started, startling Lark in the process, as neither one of them had spoken for a good five minutes. He laughed softly before continuing, "What are we doing this summer?" he asked eagerly.

"About that, I have some bad news." Lark frowned. "I'm going away for the summer, and I'm going to a place that doesn't allow phones, so I won't be able to see or talk to you for a few months."

Theo seemed stunned. "I don't get it. Where are you going that won't let you have a phone?"

"It's complicated and I'd rather not talk about it. But I'll be home in time for the first day of school, so that's good." she offered, giving a forced side smile.

"Does it have anything to do with the other week?" he asked, his face full of sincerity.

Lark darted her eyes away from the screen and frowned. "I said I'd rather not talk about it. Now, can we move on? Please?" she begged.

"Yeah, I'm sorry. I just don't know what I'm gonna do for three months."

"You could binge-watch *Supernatural*. That's gonna take some time."

He laughed at her efforts to ease his sadness. "Yeah, maybe I'll do that." He paused and then smiled. "Or maybe I'll binge-watch *Life in the Dreamhouse*. I mean, after all, that's what you did when I ignored you that one week for totaling my electric scooter."

"I don't care what you say, that show is peak entertainment." she huffed.

They talked and laughed for several more hours, at one point mamó came into Lark's room to properly wish her goodnight, then they both decided to hang up and go to bed.

"Alright, I'm going to bed. See you in the funny pages." Theo yawned.

"Night," she responded, clicking the end button.

After hanging up the phone, Lark went straight to bed, but Theo stayed up. He layed in bed and stared up at the ceiling, unable to do anything but wonder where Lark was going, and why she couldn't tell him about it. After all, they told each other everything that mattered, why was this any different? What was so big that she had to keep secrets?

By the time they had both woken up for school the next morning, neither one remembered Lark's bad news about leaving for the summer. They were too worried about having to dodge their tormentor for another week that they couldn't be bothered to think about anything else. There was really nothing about Lark or Theo that was bad enough to make them primary targets for bullying, but then again, there's not really anything bad enough about anyone that justifies them getting bullied. But still, if you have even the slightest difference about yourself that shys you away from society's definition of normal, people will call you out on it. Unfortunately, both Lark and Theo had differences that people felt calling them out on. Theo had a lisp. Not a heavy one, in fact, Lark didn't even notice it anymore, but it was there, and that was all that mattered. What separated Lark from "normal" was her neurodivergence. She had ADHD and dyslexia, and sometimes she couldn't tell the tone people were speaking in.

They stepped into school and looked at each other, both their eyes saying, "Let's hope we can get to math without a run-in." And so they dashed toward the stairs, trying their best to make it look like they weren't deliberately running away from something, or, more specifically, someone. However, since they were too busy looking down and avoiding eye contact, they didn't see Aidan Tercel, their harasser, and his foot get in the way just in time for Theo to trip on the last step.

"Oops, better watch where you're going next time, Thhheo." he sneered.

Theo didn't even try to make a snarky remark in return; instead, he just picked himself up and attempted to keep on walking. Nonetheless, Aidan wasn't finished yet, so he walked right up to the both of them and lightly shoved them against the useless wall of lockers, used by only those who signed up for one.

"What's the hurry guys? Let's hang out and talk for a while." he grinned.

"Piss off, okay? I just wanna get to class." Theo mumbled, rolling his eyes.

"What'd you sssssay, Theo?" Aidan questioned, mocking Theo's impediment and spitting in their faces in the process.

"Why can't you just leave us alone? Have you seriously got nothing better to do?" Lark asked, finally making her way into the conversation and capturing Aidan's attention.

"Hey Lark, I almost forgot about you for a second. I liked your presentation in class the other day. I thought it was really funny how you couldn't read the words even though you were the one that wrote it. Or was it supposed to be more sad and tragic than funny?"

She didn't say anything in response. Instead, she just looked at him, her face tightening and fists balling up, ready to throw the first punch. He noticed and felt the need to comment.

"Aw, Lark, are you gonna hit me? I didn't think you had the attention span to be mad at me for more than a second. After all, you're the only person I know who forgets what she was trying to say two seconds after she starts speaking."

At this point she was furious. Her skin was red and her blood was boiling. She knew his insults weren't clever in the slightest, but they were meant to attack something about them that they couldn't control, and that's all that mattered. So, in turn, she was ready to strike at any given moment. Yet her anger only egged him on.

"Go on, do it. Hit me, you won't. Your mom raised you better. It's too bad she's not around to see you chicken out, though."

That was the final straw. She lunged at him, tackling him to the ground and hitting him square in the nose and jaw until her knuckles began to bleed and a teacher pulled them apart.

"You're insane!" he shouted as another teacher helped him up, wiping the blood from his seemingly broken nose. He seemed mad and afraid of her at the same time.

"Damn straight." she smiled proudly in reply.

"Lark Byrne, go to the AP office now!" shouted the teacher, still aiding Aidan and his excessive bleeding.

Lark shrugged in response and made her way down to the office. She wasn't scared of what was going to happen to her. I mean, it was the last week of school, it's not like it could be that bad. Besides, this was her first time getting in trouble. She wasn't afraid of what could happen with mamó either. In fact, she was almost excited to tell her. Mamó had a temper too, so she'd be proud of Lark for sticking up for herself, no matter how she did it.

As she stepped into the office, the secretary looked at her with a puzzled face.

"Can I help you, sweetie?" she smiled, although she seemed quite confused. She obviously didn't think Lark was capable of breaking any rules bad enough to get her sent down.

"Yeah, I was sent down here by Miss Debilzen."

11

The secretary looked taken aback for a split second, but then her face returned to normal. It was almost as if she was saying, "What did I expect? There are no decent kids anymore." without actually having to say it. "Alright. Wait here for Mr. Siebert." she finally said.

Lark sat down and did as she was told. Almost no time had passed when Mr. Siebert came out of his office, his gray hair in disarray and his wide yet small rectangular glasses practically falling off the edge of his oblong nose. He was a tall and skinny man without a single intimidating bone in his body. He looked like the irrelevant middle-aged male extra in every generic movie.

"Lark?" he questioned.

She stood up and walked toward him, every stride she took added more tension to the room, but she was unaffected. As a matter of fact, I think getting sent to the AP office was like a big ego boost for her. She didn't like being known as the quiet little smart girl who didn't seem the type to swear, or have a short temper, or listen to rock music. She liked feeling a little rebellious, even if it only lasted a second or two.

As she sat down in the ornate chair across from Mr. Siebert's surprisingly small desk, she looked up at him, bored as ever, as if she didn't have the slightest care in the world about what he was to say next.

"You've never been sent here before. In fact, I don't think I've ever seen you at all. Why change that during the last week of school?" he asked, giving her a patronizing look that sent her blood to a simmer. She didn't take it, though. "I was tired of being pushed around," she responded glumly, playing with a loose thread on the bottom hem of her shirt.

"Then why didn't you tell someone, Lark? Physical aggression isn't the answer here."

"I have told people. Ever since freshman year I've been telling my teachers about it. About how I get bullied for the way my mind works. And it's not just me! My best friend's mom calls the school practically every month, yelling about how he comes home with cuts and bruises, or in tears because people make fun of his speech impediment. It's not fair! We've been treated like garbage for two years and nothing happens to the kid who does it, then the one time I stand up for myself, you call me down here and try to give me a lecture on *my* behavior? That doesn't make any sense." she yelled, almost forgetting that she was talking to a so-called "superior".

"Hey, I need you to lower your voice and calm down. I'll get to Aidan's punishment in a second, but right now you're the

13

one who's here because whether it was self-defense or not, you struck first." He inhaled deeply for a moment, rubbing his temples and then continuing, "Now, since this is the first time you've been in here, and considering it's the last week of school, I'm willing to let you go with three days of in-school suspension and a call to your house."

"Good luck with that." she softly laughed.

"Excuse me?" he questioned, assuming her last comment was out of disrespect.

"No, I think it's fair, and I'll take the ISS, it's just, I live with my grandma and she doesn't speak a lick of English."

"Well then I'll just send a note and you can translate it. Sound good?" he asked, tired of the conversation.

"Yep, sounds good," she replied, happy that she got off so easily.

She stepped out of his office, his note in her hand and a grin on her face. She felt accomplished; and even though she knew that Aidan would probably get off as easy as she did and that after today things were going to go back to the way they were, she still felt proud about what she had said, and especially about what she had done. It was a bit vile, but she enjoyed seeing the look on Aidan's face when she finally pushed back.

After school, Lark and Theo hopped on their bikes and rode back to his house, laughing about the earlier events of the day.

"Man, I still can't believe you got off that easy. I mean, you broke his nose!"

"I know, wasn't that great?" she smiled.

"Yeah, great. Unexpected and kinda scary, but also great." he smiled back.

When they got to Theo's house, they did the same thing they always did. They had a quick after-school snack, watched a little TV, played poker (which Lark dominated in, as usual), listened to music, and Lark went home. And they did this every day that week, until the last day of school. That was the day they were both dreading because, with Aidan temporarily off their backs, they both had time to remember Lark's mystery summer trip. Theo tried as hard as he could to get the destination out of her, but she was a closed book when it came to that subject. It was almost like she was embarrassed, or maybe scared of it. Like, she didn't want to go just as much as Theo didn't want her to.

Needless to say, though, their feelings about the situation didn't change it. Lark had to leave, end of story. So when the day finally came, they both had to buck up and accept it. Lark was all packed, although she didn't really need her stuff where she was going. I guess it was just for dramatic effect. Theo had stopped over to say his final goodbyes to her.

She said goodbye to mamó first, hugging her tightly and then saying, "Slán Mamó, is breá liom tú." (Goodbye Mamó, I love you.) She looked at Lark, tears in her eyes, and said back, "Aireoidh mé uaim thú banphrionsa." (I'll miss you princess.) By the time Lark got to Theo, they were both practically crying. Before saying anything, she wrapped her arms around him tightly, burying her face into the crook of his neck. He hugged her back, lightly stroking her hair as he looked down at her, his glasses almost falling off his face.

"I'm gonna miss you so much," he said, breaking apart from the hug.

"I'm gonna miss you so much more," she replied, a slight laugh escaping her lips.

"I doubt it."

"Hey," she said, grabbing his face and making him look at her, "we're gonna get through this. Three months can't tear us apart. You just have to promise me that when I come back, you'll still be my best friend."

"Of course I will. We're Lark and Theo forever, remember?"

"Yeah. Lark and Theo forever."

She stepped up into the large SUV and looked at him through the window. They both mouthed, "I love you." simultaneously, which should have made this departure a little less bittersweet, but all it did was make it harder for the two of them. Perhaps it would have been easier to leave if she would have known what she was going to come home to. Or perhaps if she knew that, she wouldn't have wanted to leave at all.

Part Two

"Theo, get up! Lark's coming home today!" Theo's mother shouted, causing him to jolt awake. He sat up, rubbing his eyes and looking down, realizing he had fallen asleep in his outfit from the previous day. But then again, he had been doing that a lot lately. Sometimes he'd get home late at night, well past curfew, and flop down onto his bed, no regard for what his moms would say, and fall asleep just like that.

He groaned and got out of bed, throwing off his sneakers, which he had also slept in, and walked toward his mirror. As he looked at himself, he couldn't help but wonder what Lark would think about his new look and his new way of life. After all, she had been gone for three months, which doesn't sound like a lot at first, but he hadn't been doing much at all until the last month or so, so to him it felt like an eternity. However, despite there being many things to worry about, he couldn't worry for too long, because it had just dawned on him that he'd also slept in his contacts.

He ran to the bathroom, where there was better light and was thankful to find that neither of his contacts were stuck in his eyes. So, after getting ready and putting on an outfit a little too similar to the one he had just taken off, he went into the kitchen to get breakfast. However, to his surprise and dismay, there was nothing for him on the counter.

"Hey mom, where's my breakfast?"

"We're going out for breakfast and we're taking Lark and her grandma with us. Get in the car, Eema's already waiting for you," she answered smiling.

Eema is what Theo calls his other mom. He calls her this because it's the Hebrew word for mother, and they're heavily descended from Jewish ancestors.

"Okay." he sighed, heading toward the kitchen door which led to their two-car garage.

It's not like he wasn't excited to see Lark, because trust me, ever since the day she left all he wanted to do was see her, but his nerves were taking over. You see, the summer changed Theo, both inside and out. When Lark left, he felt scared and vulnerable to the outside world, so he let it change him instead of showing it who the real him was. It was quite cowardly, but it was his only defense. Blend in, at all costs.

Ironically, what he saw about the world was that most people considered normal don't actually care about what other people think, or at least that's what they want you to believe. Unfortunately, by this time he had already made his transformation; so the Theo he wasn't afraid to show off, wasn't really him. It was an alter-ego by the name of...

"Spade!" a young boy shouted.

"Oh, hey Elio," Theo answered, slightly waving at the boy as he stepped into the small restaurant.

"Hello, welcome to Citrus Cafe, how can I help you?" an overly cheerful hostess asked as Theo and his moms stepped through the door.

"We called ahead, Veksler, party of five." his Eema told the lady. She flipped through her binder, which seemed mostly blank, until she found it.

"Okay, right this way." she smiled, grabbing five menus and leading them toward a table in the back. Half of it was a booth, and the other half was like a regular table. Theo slid into the booth side while his moms sat in the chairs.

"So Theo, why did that boy call you Spade?" his mom asked.

"Uh, it's a long story. I'd rather not get into i-" He stopped mid-sentence and his breath hitched. There she stood. The beautiful young girl he called his best friend. She was staring off into space, a normal thing for her to do, and smiling. She was wearing a flowy light blue dress with tiny white daisies on it, something she had obviously been forced into wearing. He figured that if it were up to her, she would've worn ripped jeans and a Black Sabbath shirt. By the looks of it, the only part of her ensemble she got a say about was her shoes. They were her white Converse high-tops, stained dark beige from the mud.

When she saw him her smile grew from slight to bigger than the length of Saturn's rings stretched out. As the waitress led her and mamó to the table, she grew impatient and dashed toward it, sliding into the booth and giving him a hug. He hugged back tighter, thanking the heavens that she was finally back. When they pulled apart they realized that Theo's moms and mamó were staring at them.

"You sure missed each other, huh?" Theo's mom asked, laughing softly.

"What, y'all didn't miss me?" Lark asked, also laughing.

Theo's mom grinned before saying, "Wow. I haven't heard someone say y'all in a while. My sister-in-law says it, but I haven't seen her in a few years." She seemed sad at first, but then she smiled again, reminiscing about her childhood in Idaho while the others sat in silence. "Oh, how rude of us, we haven't properly met." She turned to Lark, signifying that she wanted her to translate that to mamó. "I'm Missy, and this is my wife Delilah." Mamó looked at them after Lark had finished speaking and smiled. Mamó was always supportive of all people,

21

which was pretty rare for her generation. She said she believed that if two people loved each other, any two people, then it was nobody else's business to tell them they were wrong.

"Alright, I know I've only been back for, like, three seconds, but I can't ignore the elephant in the room forever." Lark paused and turned to Theo. "What's up with your new look? I mean it's cool, don't get me wrong, but what happened to Theodore Gray? You look like the lovechild of a greaser and an 80s bad-boy stereotype."

She was right. His once short and feathered golden blonde hair had grown out to the end of his neck and dyed jet black. He now also had bangs that were gelled together in small sections and fell in front of his forehead, almost covering his eyes. His round glasses had been replaced with contacts, colored to make his hazel eyes appear deep indigo. He had also pierced his ears. Both had diamond studs and the right one had an orbital and rook as well. His wardrobe was completely different, too. It looked like he took a razor to his American Eagle jeans and put his t-shirts through a shredder. It seemed as if the only clothing of his he hadn't ripped apart was his leather jacket. He looked cool to her, but out of place in terms of the century.

"He does, doesn't he?" Delilah replied, giggling.

"Yeah," Theo began, "I don't know, I guess Theodore Gray wanted to go back to the Victorian days."

"Right, so you decided to jump ahead a hundred years and become Theo Cruise instead?" Lark joked.

"Actually, I hear it's Spade now," Missy remarked.

"Spade? Where'd they get that one from? A deck of cards?" Lark sneered.

Theo turned red from embarrassment and rolled his eyes, only half playfully. Lark had been gone for so long, he didn't think it was fair of her to judge him when she wasn't there to stop his change of facade.

"No, believe it or not, it actually has a meaning." he retorted, pretending to read the menu.

"Care to share it, then?" she asked, trying to divert his attention away from the menu.

"Maybe later."

The rest of their time at the cafe was spent in near silence, except for the occasional "How is everything?" from the waitress and the subtle, "Fine, thank you.'"s from the table. No one dared to ask Theo about his new persona, or Lark about her trip. They just stared at their food and tried not to upset anyone. And when they were done eating, Missy and Delilah picked up the check, thanked Lark and Mamó for coming, took Theo, and left.

On the car ride home, Missy turned to Theo and asked, "How was it? Seeing Lark again, that is."

"Different. I mean, she seemed the same, but I guess that's why I was a little bothered," he answered.

"What do you mean, hun?" Delilah asked back.

"She never did like change, and she never liked hiding her opinions either. I just hoped that she'd keep an open mind this time. You know, for me." he sighed.

"I'm sure she'll come around, baby. Just give her some time." Missy smiled.

He smiled back to humor her, but inside he was stuck wondering why Lark was acting the way she was. She had just gotten back from a three-month-long excursion and made it out to seem like nothing was out of the ordinary. I mean, she could have at least said how things went. She didn't have to tell them where she was, just how it was being there. He really hoped it didn't have anything to do with the incident that occurred a few weeks before she left.

The next day was a day that Theo had been both looking forward to and dreading since the first day of summer break. He had been looking forward to it because it was going to be the first full day he'd get to spend with Lark again, but he was dreading it because he had to go back to school. He wasn't worried about Aidan anymore, because, let's just say, he took care of him this summer. No, he was worried about what everyone would think of "Spade". I mean, he had become him to please everyone and try to meet their standards, but even Lark didn't seem to like him, which really raised his nerves.

He had to shake it off, though, because Spade didn't worry about what other people thought; then again, Spade didn't worry about anything. As he got on his bike and peddled to Lark's, he tried to think of the best way to tell her how he got his new look and his new name. The truth was partly bold and partly pathetic, but it was what Lark would want to hear, so it was his best shot.

He barely reached her driveway before she sped past him on her bike, calling out, "Haha, too slow!" from behind her. When he caught up to her, she had her feet on the handlebars next to her hands. She smiled at him as he called her crazy, nodding in agreement. She finally returned to the normal position and turned to him, looking him dead in the eyes and saying, "Theodore Wells Veksler." He looked at her and answered, "Lark Legacy Byrne. Alright, now that we've established we both have names, can we move on?"

"I'm just trying to figure out how they got Spade from that."

"Oh, yeah, that." he answered, pretending like he didn't know this would be brought up and not wanting to go on. "So, you remember Aidan, right?"

She sighed. "How could I forget?"

"He's kinda the one who got me that name."

"Wait, are you saying you're friends with him or something?" she asked, a little too loudly, furrowing her brows.

"God no, Lark! That's not what I meant," he replied back anxiously.

"Then what did you mean?" Her patience was coming to an end.

"Well, one day in about the middle of July, Aidan came to my house. I'm not sure why exactly, it seemed like he just wanted to push me around a little for kicks. So anyway, he came into my backyard while I was doing some yard work for my moms, and he started saying some things, and I just got so tired of it. It was like you the day you broke his nose. I just couldn't take it anymore, so, when he was getting ready to punch me or push me or whatever it was he was gonna do, I picked up the

spade that was next to me and I hit him over the head with it."
He breathed out, nervous about what she was going to say but
happy he finally got it off his chest.

"What did you do to him?" she asked, actually seeming
concerned, for some reason.

"He got a concussion and was sent to the hospital. I told
the cops it was self-defense since it technically was, so I didn't
get in a lot of trouble for it. Ever since then people have been
calling me Spade. I'd probably be happier about it if Aidan
wasn't out to get me. But now that I got you here with me, I
don't really have to worry, do I?" he smiled. Although his
question was rhetorical, he was still a bit sad when she just
stared at him blankly.

"Your lisp," she said finally.

"Huh?" he asked.

"Your lisp," she repeated. "It's gone. I can't believe I just
noticed that."

"Oh, yeah. My moms put me through speech therapy this
summer. I guess I finally got tired of it." he said dully.

"You mean you finally got tired of Aidan making fun of it.
I know you liked it, Theo. You thought it made you kinda
special. Hell, *I* thought it made you kinda special. But, if you say
you wanted it gone, I believe you." she smiled. He smiled back,

glad she reacted quite well to the whole situation, even though she never *really* said what she thought of it.

"There's just one more question I had, though." He raised an eyebrow as if asking what the question was without saying it. "Why'd you change your look?"

His smile faded. "It's pretty stupid, so promise you won't laugh." She sighed and drew a cross over her heart, and then held up three fingers (for scout's honor). "After everyone started calling me Spade, I saw it as a chance to renew myself. I liked Theodore Gray, don't get me wrong, but I didn't really think anyone else would, so I turned into what I thought Spade would look like. You know, someone cool. Someone you'd see in the halls and be a little afraid of. I just wanted people to know that I couldn't be pushed around anymore, so I thought if I looked tougher, they'd believe it. I know it sounds stupid bu-"

"No, I get it." Lark interrupted.

"You do?" he asked, completely flabbergasted.

"Yeah. You were so scared of people judging you for who you are, so you turned into someone people would be afraid to judge. Kind of like the real Dorian Gray. I get it. I don't agree with it, but I get it." she responded, riding off on her bike and ignoring his calls after her.

When he got to school, her bike was already chained up and she was halfway up the stairs. He tried to catch up to her, but the wave of people held him back. By the time he got to first hour, she was sitting at her desk and staring at the floor. He walked up beside her and tried to sit down, but someone was already at the desk adjacent to her.

"Get up," he said to the kid at the desk.

"What?" the kid asked.

"You heard me. Get up. Now, before I beat you to a pulp." he jived.

The kid stood up a little too quickly, as he tripped over his own two feet, then he got back up and ran to a different desk. Theo took a seat and looked indifferent as he turned his attention back to Lark.

"What was that?" she asked, not believing what she'd just witnessed.

"What?" Theo counterasked, not seeing any problem with his behavior.

"You just threatened that kid over a desk. What's the matter with you?"

"He was in my seat. Besides, he probably had it coming. Anyway, are you good? Because you said some pretty untrue things earlier. I mean, I'm not afraid. It was kinda rude of you to say it, too."

She stared at him in shock before scoffing and turning away. He sat there in confused amazement. Why was she being like this? He didn't think he'd done anything to deserve an attitude like that from her.

They didn't talk for the rest of the day. Half of it was because Lark was pissed at Theo for being a jerk, and the other half was because Theo was mad at Lark for being mad at him. It's all pretty childish if you ask me. However, their anger had to come to an end at some point, because they were still best friends. Lark was stubborn, so she wouldn't try to make amends first, that was just a given. And since Theo was both in the wrong and more tired of being mad, he was the first to crack.

"Lark!" he called out. She looked over her shoulder before turning back to her bike lock. "Lark!" he yelled again. She rolled her eyes and called back, "What?" He seemed pleased that she even acknowledged him, so he took advantage of it. "Lark, I'm sorry, okay? I know I've been a jerk today, and I'm sorry. Are we good now?" he asked, his eyes pleading for her to say yes. "Sure," she said, stuffing the lock into her backpack. "Really?" he asked. "Yeah, why not?" she answered. Theo didn't seem to realize that she was being sarcastic, so he acted as if everything was normal again.

As they rode home, he kept trying to make small talk with her, and she kept ignoring him, until finally, she was tired of it. "What do you want, Theo?" she yelled.

"I want you to talk to me!" he yelled back. "You haven't done that in a long time."

"What do you want me to say?" she asked.

"Anything!"

"No, you wanna know something. If you didn't you would've shut up and let me be mad at you. So what is it?"

"I wanna know where you went this summer! I know you don't wanna talk about it, but I do. I just want you to trust me enough to tell me!" he replied.

"Fine, Theo! You wanna know where I went this summer? I went to Laurel Creek, okay! Are you happy now?"

"Lark, why did you go to Laurel Creek?" he asked slowly, fearing he knew what she would say next.

"Don't ask questions you already know the answer to." she sighed.

He nodded, knowing exactly what she had gone there for. Even though he had hoped and prayed that her trip had nothing to do with it, in the end a small part of him always knew that it had everything to do with the incident.

Part Three

Laurel Creek was the psychiatric ward just north of town. Theo and Lark used to think only major nutcases went to wards. They knew better now. Lark wasn't sick, and she wasn't crazy to the point where you can't function right, she was just a little weird. But after the incident, it didn't matter what she said, all that mattered was that mamó wanted her to get better, at any cost. Somehow she thought throwing her fifteen-year-old granddaughter into an asylum would help her, and I suppose it did, but it was really hard for Lark to come to terms with. She hated that she had to go to begin with, but it was even worse knowing that mamó thought she was bad enough to have to go at all. But who could blame her? Anyone who saw what she saw on the day of Lark's incident probably would have sent her there too.

It was a breezy Friday afternoon. Lark had just come home from school, trying to hide her tears of frustration from mamó and almost succeeding, if only she hadn't forgotten to take her shoes off at the front door, she never would have had to turn around and come face-to-face with her. "Cad atá mícheart? Cén fáth a bhfuil tú ag gol?" (What's wrong? Why are you

33

crying?) she asked. "Rud ar bith, Mamó. Nílim ach beagáinín craiceáilte faoin scoil." (Nothing, Mamó. I'm just a little mad about school.) Lark said back. She knew Lark was lying, or at least not telling the whole truth, but she thought it would be best to let her cool down for a while. This is now one of her biggest regrets.

Lark usually saved her showers for nighttime. There was no reason, it was just always something she had done. However, today she took one as soon as she put her bag down and took her shoes off. At first, Mamó didn't think anything of it and turned on the TV. She fell asleep to it, so she didn't realize that Lark had been in the bathroom for three hours until Theo's obnoxious doorbell ringing interrupted her sleep. She jolted awake and answered the front door. Theo knew a little bit of Gaelic (about enough to have small talk with mamó), so he said, "Halò, a bheil Lark timcheall? Bha còir aice a thighinn a-null airson dinnear." (Hey, is Lark around? She was supposed to come over for dinner.) Mamó furrowed her brows and then dashed to the stairs, a confused yet urgent Theo following close behind.

"Lark? Lark!" mamó yelled. When she didn't answer she called again. Within seconds mamó's patience ran out and she went up the stairs. After seeing that the light was still on, she knocked on the bathroom door, calling out her name again. Theo looked at her and said, "I'm gonna try to break down the door. Is that okay?" When she gave him a blank stare, he smacked himself upside the head. "Right, you can't understand me. Let's see here." He proceeded to make gestures, trying to explain what he was going to do, seeing as he didn't know how to say it. For a while it seemed as though she understood him and was okay with it, so he broke down the door, which wasn't hard considering the wood was weak and the hinges were rusting. When she looked at him in slight anger and confusion, he realized he may have not been the best at their crazy and frantic game of charades.

But she couldn't be mad anymore, not after what she saw when she looked past him and into the bathtub. There lied her beautiful granddaughter in a full tub, head below water, not moving a muscle. She broke down and cried, screaming out and not knowing what to do. Thankfully, Theo and Lark were in a health class and they had just had their CPR unit. He grabbed her still fully-clothed body out of the tub, ignoring all the water splashing onto him and the floor, and set her down on the rug, checking for a pulse. His heart was racing, but he knew he had to stay calm. He set one of his hands on top of the other, intertwining his fingers and pumping on her chest thirty times,

35

then he turned to her and opened her mouth, lifting her chin up and pinching her nostrils. He breathed in twice before going back to the chest compressions. It went on like this for six minutes, and they thought she was gone. Then, when he went to give her one last rescue breath, her eyes opened.

She spat water out and started coughing like crazy. When she was done, she turned to Theo and started sobbing uncontrollably. In all their years of being friends, he'd never once seen her break like this. His entire body went numb at the sight, and he started crying right there with her. They latched onto each other as if it was the last time they'd ever get the chance to. "I wasn't strong enough, Theo. I just wasn't strong enough." she bawled. He cupped her face in his hands and looked into her eyes. "Don't say that Lark. Don't you ever say that. You're the strongest person I know. You just got tired, that's all. And it's okay, because I'm tired too. I'm so damn tired, but we can get through it. Because we're Lark and Theo forever, right?" Their breathing had evened out more, but their tears were still falling fast, like raindrops on a car window. "Right." she answered. "Lark and Theo forever."

That was the last time Mamó left Lark alone. She wouldn't leave her side unless she knew Theo was there. She thought sending her to the ward over summer break could help her, though. That maybe they'd do things for her there that she'd never even think to do. And I suppose it did help. Lark no longer thought about those things, but then again, that could've been because she was too preoccupied with trying to understand why Theo was going through a fifth-life crisis. But she did seem happier, and that was all that really mattered.

When they got to Lark's house, instead of continuing on to his house like he usually did, Theo turned into her driveway and dropped his bike next to hers. He looked up at her and looked away when she met his eyes.

"I'm sorry for asking. I'm sorry for everything, really, but most recently for asking where you were instead of shutting up and realizing you weren't telling me for a reason." He spoke in a low, calm voice.

"I'm sorry for snapping at you and not telling you sooner. I just didn't want you to think I was some weirdo nut job. I'm also sorry for never properly thanking you for saving my life. I'm actually really happy you did." She stopped and laughed softly, obviously uncomfortable with the serious turn the conversation had taken. Then she looked up and smiled. "Besides, I don't think I would've wanted to miss you turning into Spade. I mean, he's got Dinger Holfield's style, Johnny

Cade's looks, and Dallas Winston's personality. What's not to like?"

He laughed along before stopping abruptly. "Wait, Dallas Winston's a jerk."

"Yeah, that's the point." she called, stepping through her front doorway. He stood in her driveway for a minute or two, wondering if she actually thought he was turning into a jerk. I mean, he sure didn't think he was. He thought he was surviving the best way he knew how to: being aggressive. Being like Aidan...

The next day, as Lark and Theo were chaining their bikes up, they heard many low whispers and saw dozens of pairs of eyes staring directly at Theo, or more so, staring at Spade. No one would have ever stared at Theo, because no one knew of his existence, and he used to like it that way. But not Spade. Everyone knew Spade, and he loved being the center of attention, regardless of whether it was good or bad attention he was getting. As he walked with Lark to class, he acted as if he didn't see the crowds of people looking at him, he also acted like he didn't care. But Lark could see the smirk on his face and the look of pride in his eyes. She knew better than to ask him, but she wondered why they were all whispering. They hadn't done it yesterday, and, as far as she knew, he hadn't done anything worthy of discussion since the eighth period bell rang.

Then she saw it. They both did. The reason why all the kids were talking. He strode toward them, a nefarious look of vengefulness on his odious and grimaced face, which now sported a large, diagonal, and not to mention very visible, scar on the right side of his forehead and a crooked nose. As he drew nearer, Lark's breath hitched and went shaky. Even though she had beat the tar out of him, it didn't change the fact that Aidan was her bully, and he had said some things that would stick with her for a very long time, if not the rest of her life. She looked over at Theo to see how he was doing, but Theo wasn't there anymore. In his place was Spade, who looked cool and unbothered at his presence. This somewhat uneased her. When he had finally reached them, he looked Spade up and down before chortling at his appearance. He was obviously as impressed with his new looks as he would've been with a pile of old shoes.

"Hey, Theo, I think you and I have some things to talk about." he spat, looking up into his eyes. It was kind of hard for Theo to be intimidated by him now that he had grown an extra four inches and practically towered over him. Being a late bloomer had finally come to his advantage.

"It's Spade." he said coolly.

Aidan laughed and seemed unimpressed. "Fine then, I have some things to discuss with you, 'Spade'. Like how you're gonna pay for giving me this." he scorned, pointing to his scar.

"You should be thanking me. It draws the attention away from your messed up nose. It makes you look tougher, too. You know, like you actually get into fights and you're not all talk."

"Oh yeah? Well, how's this for talk?" he asked. Before anyone could have a reaction, Aiden hit Spade square in the jaw with a right hook. He rubbed it for a second before looking down at Aidan and giving him a wary look. "You don't wanna get into this with me," he warned. "Oh, I think I do." Aidan said back smiling. Spade sighed before slowly moving his hand toward his back pocket. "Alright, man. But just remember, you asked for this." He pulled a switchblade out from his back jean pocket and flicked it open. Aidan's confident look turned to a cowardly one faster than the blade had left the handle. Spade got real close to Aidan's face and started to whisper, "Now I suggest you leave before things start to get scary." Aidan slowly backed up and turned around to sprint away as soon as he had gotten far enough down the hall.

Spade turned the blade back into the handle and put the knife away as if nothing had happened. And then, Theo was back. He took notice of Lark's fearful expression and became worried.

"What's wrong?" he asked.

"What do you mean 'What's wrong?' Did you not see what you just did?" she replied, her voice slightly cracking every few words.

"Yeah? So what? I was just scaring him."

"He didn't know that. Nobody else knew that. And you know what? I don't even think you knew that. I think you were just waiting to see if he'd actually back down." she said, turning from fearful to angry.

"Lark, you didn't think I'd actually cut him, did you?" He was beginning to be the fearful one.

"I didn't think *you* would, but I wouldn't question it from Spade."

"I am Spade." he responded puzzled.

"No you're not, Theo! I know you're practically blind, but I thought even you'd be able to see that." she muttered.

Then, she walked away. He thought about going after her so they could talk it out, but there didn't seem to be a point, so he let her go. She spent the rest of the day in a numb state, trying her best to figure out what had happened to the Theo she knew, and how she could get him back. Meanwhile, he spent the rest of the day in pure agony. He missed having her next to him. Whispering funny things in his ear in the middle of class, slinging her arm around his shoulders in the halls, pretending to read his palm whenever he got bored. But most of all, he missed her poems. He supposed he hadn't heard one in a while because they were about Theodore Gray, but he hoped that maybe Spade could get a poem. Wishful thinking seemed to be a curse all of Theo's characters carried.

Over the next few weeks, Lark and Theo kept their distance. He didn't want to be apart from her, but he knew better than to be around Lark when she was mad. But the thing he couldn't realize at the time was that she wasn't mad. She was actually in mourning. No person had died, per se, but it was still a great loss to her. She had finally come to terms with the fact that Theodore Gray was to stay in the Victorian era, and Spade was here to stay for the foreseeable future. It was hard for her to keep away from him as well, because for whatever reason she still had hope that somewhere buried deep underneath the cold and belligerent exterior of Spade, Theo still lived on. More wishful thinking.

One day, while unchaining her bike from after school, Lark caught Theo gazing in her direction. This had caught her off guard, so instead of smiling or waving, she looked down at her feet quickly. She felt bad for this, but at the same time, she didn't think this would affect him much, considering he hadn't tried to speak to her within the past few weeks either. However, her curiosity got the best of her and she raised her head up again, hoping he'd still be looking her way. To her surprise, he was actually coming towards her, dragging his bike along with him. She didn't know what to do, so she just stood there waiting for him to arrive.

As he made his last stride toward her, he looked her up and down before delicately saying, "Hey."

"Hey." she said back. "Did you need something?"

He looked startled for a second and then frowned. "Oh, uh, nope. I just wanted to see how you've been. We haven't really talked since... well, you know, you were there too." He laughed nervously as he scratched the back of his neck and gulped, a bit louder than expected.

She noticed but ignored it, and instead continued their conversation. "Yeah. I mean, that's partially my bad. I guess I just needed some space for a bit."

"I get it." he replied, a small glum look resting upon his face.

She cleared her throat and hopped on her bike. Thinking their chat was over, he turned around and started to get on his bike, when she called out to him. "Hey," He spun around and looked at her urgently. "I wrote you a poem. It's at my house if you wanna come and get it." His expression immediately brightened as he followed her back to her house.

Although the ride was spent in complete silence, Theo enjoyed it thoroughly because he was finally with Lark again. She pulled into her driveway and didn't even check to see if he had made it before running into her house to retrieve the piece of parchment which held her latest poem on it's surface. When she returned, she handed him the paper. He was about to unfold it when she stopped him. "Do me a favor and wait until you get home. I'd rather not be here when you read it." she mumbled. He just nodded and shoved it into his pocket.

She shifted uncomfortably and he got the hint that she wanted him to leave. He uttered a quick, "Thanks." and hurried off, urging to get home and read what couldn't be read in her presence. But while he was excited, she was nervous. She wrote the poem because it's how she felt, she still loved him, and no matter who he had become, she didn't want to hurt him.

When he got home he nearly ran into every wall and doorway because of how fast he was going. He shut his bedroom door immediately and reached for the paper. He started quickly unfolding it, but made sure to be careful as to not rip the paper. As his eyes landed on the page, he realized that this poem in particular was much longer than the ones she normally wrote. Those were more like cute little limericks she made up to pass the time by. This was something she sat down and took time to write. He expected that since it was longer, it would bring him more joy, but as he read, his heart grew heavy and sunk to the bottom of his chest.

"Poor young Theodore Gray,
Lay on his bed, his mind awake
He tossed and turned
And still he yearned
For the girl he used to know.

The pretty young girl he used to know
With short auburn hair and a modern glow
The girl with a smile like all the stars
And a laugh that could send him to mars

He sat and wondered what could have been

If she knew him now and didn't know him then
Small tears streaming down each cheek
Like her, each one was delicate and meek.

'But it doesn't matter now, I suppose'
He thought while hugging onto her clothes
The ones she'd left there long ago
Back when she was the girl he used to know."

When he finished reading it, he set the paper down on his bed and fell on his back. Hot tears started streaming down his cheeks, each one falling faster than the last. And there he lay, crying alone in his dark room, thinking about exactly what the poem said he was. The girl he used to know.

Part Four

It had been a week since Lark had given Theo the poem, but to him it felt like it was only yesterday. All of his thoughts were based around it. Her words not only saddened him, but they confused him, too, considering Lark had been saying how he was the one who changed, but the poem was saying another thing. Another thing that confused him was Lark's behavior. On the day she had given him the poem, she actually spoke to him and allowed him to come back to her house, so he thought they were making progress, but since then, she hadn't only been ignoring him, but she was flat out avoiding him. She'd take the long way to her classes and run out of school as soon as the bell rang and hop on her bike just to make sure he wouldn't have time to talk to her. It didn't make any sense to him. Why was she purposely trying to stay away from him? Although he may have acted differently toward others, he was never like that to her.

At this point, life seemed like a game to beat more than like a game to enjoy. Every day he woke up, Theo felt like he was stuck in an endless cycle and the only way to break it was to bring Spade out. But that seemed pointless considering Spade didn't have anyone to play the game with. Yet, still, Spade lived on. He was like an obsession of Theo's. He couldn't always control himself or what he was doing when he was Spade; he felt like something else was taking over him, but the power he felt when he was him was something exhilarating he knew he couldn't give up.

As he walked to his class, he pushed through the halls muttering, "Get the hell out of my way." every now and then. Nowadays, bitterness seemed like a characteristic he was trying to achieve. Although, he didn't have to try very hard. Even his teachers were starting to notice it, but of course no one asked him about it. They were too swept up in their own lives to try and help, much less care. Instead, they let him turn into another school terrorist, turning the other cheek when they saw him attacking another student. They thought his new attitude was just a phase that would soon pass, and that because of that he wasn't worth helping. "Boys fight all the time, it's just their nature. It's no big deal." they thought. That would be something they'd regret thinking in the future.

After school, he noticed that Lark hadn't immediately ran off and took it to his advantage. He approached her cautiously, not wanting to startle her. It was almost like watching someone trying to approach a sleeping tiger. He didn't want to upset her, but he felt the need to get her attention. If not for a conversation then at least for an explanation as to why she had all of a sudden become the anti-Theo. He tapped her on the shoulder gently, startling her a little, but that was to be expected. She turned away as soon as she saw it was him and didn't seem like she wanted to recognize his actuality. But finally, she exhaled and uttered, "What?" in a rather impatient tone.

"I just wanted to know why you've been avoiding me. I'm not mad, I just feel like I deserve an explanation." he replied.

"I needed to clear my head and think about some things, and I knew I wouldn't be able to do that if I kept running into you. You're too much of a distraction."

"Anything you wanna talk about?" he asked, a look of concern etched on his face.

"Uh, yeah, actually." She pulled him aside so their conversation could be a bit more private. "I saw my dad this summer when I was, well, you know where." She paused to take in a shaky breath. She wasn't going to cry, you could just tell, but it seemed like the words were tough for her to say, not that that was hard to understand. "Seeing him there finally made me understand why my mom never told me anything about him. I mean, sure, he's alive, but you can tell he's been gone for a long time. The only reason I knew he was my dad was because whenever I used to ask my mom about him, she'd act like she was ignoring my questions and tell me a story about a man who lived in a place called Laurel Creek. These were usually horror stories about terrible things the man had done. Sometimes to his wife, but usually to himself. After seeing him there, it was obvious the stories were about him. He's real messed up, Theo." The whole time she was speaking, she never took her eyes off the ground. It was almost like she was talking to herself.

"I'm sorry, Lark. That's really sucky."

"Yeah, well, sucky's just how my life's been going lately." she said somberly. She got on her bike and started to peddle off before stopping briskly and looking back at him. "There's something else I wanted to say. Something else I wanted you to know." He raised an eyebrow and drew closer to her. "I know the poem makes it sound like I'm the one who changed, but our time apart helped me realize that that's because I *am* the one who changed. All your life, you've always been the same. Scared, weak, vulnerable. I know it's hard to hear, believe me, it's hard to say, but it's the truth. You've always allowed everyone around you to influence you. To mold your mind into thinking there's a specific way you're supposed to look and act, but there's not. It's just not like that, Theo. Hell, you even did that with me." When he shot her a muddled look she continued.

"Haven't you ever noticed that you always refer to yourself as Spade or Theodore Gray? You've never once said 'me' when talking about yourself, but that's because you never *were* talking about yourself. You've been so afraid to show the world who you really are, that I'm not sure even you know who that is. Instead you turn yourself into these characters and play the parts because you think that's the only way people are going to like you, and that's sad because you're just plain wrong. I mean, sure, maybe Theodore Gray is the real you, and sure, maybe it's Spade. But I think it's someone so much better than them because that person is you, Theo. And not even you can take that away from yourself. So stop being afraid. Stop being someone you're not, because frankly I think everyone's tired of it."

"Oh yeah?" he questioned, trying so hard not to show how much her words had hurt him. "Well what's so different about you?"

"What's different about me is that I don't need you to live. Not anymore. A few months ago you were literally the only reason I was alive. And now look at me. This is our first real conversation in over a month, and I've been doing just fine up until now."

"My condolences. I didn't know talking to me was such a burden." he snapped.

"On the contrary, it kinda felt good getting that off my chest, so thanks for listening." she responded, not taking his attitude. She started to ride off again before hearing someone shout, and although it wasn't directed toward her, she still wanted to stick around for the discussion.

"Hey Spade!" Aidan yelled, his raspy voice breaking slightly. He turned and glared at him. "You didn't think I'd forget about you, did you? You hit me with a shovel, and you pulled a blade on me. That's not something I'm just gonna forget. And it's *definitely* not something I'm gonna forgive. We have some things to hash out, and this time you can't pull anything to scare me away, because I'm willing to risk some blood so long as you get what's coming to you in the end." he snickered. His lips curled into a devious and wretched grin that sent shivers up Theo's spine.

"I don't wanna fight you, Aidan." he whispered.

"No no no," he laughed, blowing his dark bangs out of his face. "You're not getting out of this. You see, as far as I'm concerned, you can change your looks, and your name, and the way you act, but deep down, you're always gonna be that same scared little lisp-ridden boy you've always been. It's who you are, and no matter what, you can't run away from that. All I'm trying to do is prove just that, and I don't care which version of you I have to fight to do it."

Theo gulped and looked down. The last thing he wanted to do was fight Aidan. He wasn't afraid of him at all, he just didn't think fighting would solve anything. Maybe temporarily, but in the end he and Aidan would always have bad blood between them. But he knew better than to back down from a fight, so he nodded and said, "Okay. But not here."

Aidan seemed mad at first, but after consideration, he realized that Theo was right. Fighting on school grounds was more than stupid, it was just plain reckless. They could be torn apart at any second and punished. But if they did it off grounds, the school couldn't really do anything about it. Not unless someone tried to press charges behind the other's back. They decided it would be better to meet by the rock quarry around eight that night. It wouldn't be a private affair, though. Dozens of kids who had been listening to the parley decided that they wanted to see the live show. Spade Vs. Aidan, One Night Only. Lark was one of these kids. Condoning fights was against her better judgement, but she wanted to see someone besides herself finally stand up to Aidan, and who better than her ex-best friend, his second most targeted victim.

After making all the arrangements and coming up with a fair set of rules (no weapons, no biting, no groin hits, no fish hooking, no eye gouging etc.) they all went home, awaiting eight o'clock with a nervous excitement. At Theo's house, he desperately stabbed his dinner, not even making an attempt to eat it. He was too frazzled to do anything other than count down the minutes until eight. At the moment, it was sixty-six.

"Theo?" his mom asked, snapping him back into reality. He hummed in response. "Why aren't you eating your dinner? Is there something wrong with it?" He eyed her and shook his head. "No, I'm just not hungry." He stayed silent for a moment then asked to be excused. His moms nodded and he dashed to his room. He locked the door and sat down on his bed, staring at the posters on his walls. "There's no way this is going to end well." he said quietly to himself.

Meanwhile at Lark's house, she was a nervous wreck. She may not have cared for Spade, but Theo was a different story. Even though she'd spent the last month convincing herself that her Theo was gone, she still wasn't completely sold on the idea. Mamó was asleep in her room, which didn't come as a surprise to Lark. She often took naps in the evening and was up and moving by three in the morning. Ever since Lark came home, mamó had given her a lot more space. She truly believed that the ward had helped her, which was good for Lark, because she was starting to feel claustrophobic in her own home.

Anyway, she was sitting in her living room, flipping through the channels on the TV when she heard her phone go off. She picked it up and saw that Theo had texted her.

"Are you coming tonight?" it read.

"Probably." she answered.

"Do you think I could win?" he asked.

"You could, but I don't know why you'd want to."

"I know you don't like fights, but do you think you could cheer me on? I'd really like the support."

"Only if you're fighting as Theo. I won't cheer for Spade."

"Good, because tonight I am fighting as Theo. The real Theo."

She smiled as she read the text. The real Theo was someone she'd been longing to meet for a while now.

At seven forty-five sharp, Theo lifted up his window, climbed up on its sill, and jumped to the ground below. Little did he know, only four blocks away, Lark was doing virtually the same thing, except she had to jump to the big willow tree next to her window and climb down from there. Surprisingly, it was actually much easier than she had anticipated. They both ran in the direction of the quarry, but never crossed paths with each other on the way. However, when they arrived, their similar journeys had become very different. As soon as people saw Theo, they were going up to him and patting him on the back, wishing him good luck and applauding him. Whereas, when people saw Lark, they just ignored her. As far as they were concerned, she was just another student who came to watch the fight, which she technically was. The only thing that made her different from the others was that she knew both the boys personally, and she wasn't there just to watch a fight for sport. She was there to watch long overdue justice be served.

By the time Theo had gotten to the edge of the crowd, he saw that Aidan was already there waiting for him. He had changed into different clothes, presumably ones he didn't care about getting blood stains on. Theo went to shake his hand, but Aidan took this as an opportunity to start the fight instead, so he grabbed Theo's wrist and twisted his arm around. Everyone in the crowd could hear his wrist snap. They all winced and made sympathetic "ooh" sounds. Even though it was a dirty move, it didn't mean Aidan was a smart or experienced fighter, Theo could tell that right away. His stance wasn't stable, so Theo swept his legs and he fell to the ground, causing him to let go of Theo's wrist. Although it was rude to kick someone while they were down, Theo didn't think he had much of a choice, so he did just that.

As Aidan stood up, everyone could hear him groaning in pain. It seemed as if the fight was over, even though it had just started. But just as Theo was about to walk away, Aidan punched him right in the gut, causing him to double over in pain. When he looked back up he charged at Aidan, tackling him to the ground. He sat on top of him swinging punches left and right. Like Lark months ago, his knuckles were bleeding. Also like Lark, he broke Aidan's nose again. At this point, blood was starting to go everywhere. On their clothes, the grass, the rocks. It even got on the shoes of some of the kids watching, and instead of being disgusted by it, they all thought it was a cool memorabilia of tonight. Eventually, Aidan got the better of Theo and got on top of him, punching his jawline multiple times before pressing his hands against his throat. He couldn't kill him, that was one of the rules. Theo supposed Aidan just wanted him to pass out, but he wasn't having it. Despite it being against their rules, he kneed Aidan in the crotch. It worked, Aidan drew his hands back, allowing Theo enough time to push him off and stand up.

Lark noticed an agitated worker from the quarry coming closer to the fight but didn't say anything. Not that it would have made a difference if she had. Those boys were going to brawl until one of them surrendered. And as he stood up, Aidan made it very clear that he would not be that boy. He wiped the blood from his face and looked up at Theo with a look of pure wrath in his eyes. He straightened himself up and put his hands to his sides. Lark wasn't sure why he did this. Perhaps it was to show that even though he was injured, his determination to win outweighed any pain he might have been feeling. And then, in the blink of an eye, Aidan went from standing up straight and completely still to lunging at Theo like a bull charging at a Matador.

And before anyone could stop it, before anyone could even realize what was going on, Aidan ran Theo, and himself, off the cliff of the rock quarry. The employee who had been approaching them quickly stopped and ran back inside, presumably to call an ambulance. All the kids who had been watching ran to the edge to see the aftermath, but not Lark. She stood in place, tears streaming down her cheeks as she took in the events of the last thirty seconds. Even though it sounds silly and stupid, she started writing a poem. Not a funny one like the ones she wrote for her Theo, and not a meaningful one like the one she wrote for Spade. This one was a sad poem, because even though it lacked length, it was powerful enough to make her cry every time she thought about it.

"Poor young Theodore Gray"

Because of the echo, you could hear them hit the ground with a loud thud. Lark screamed so loudly and powerfully it seemed as if she'd be mute by its end.

"Lay on the hospital bed"

The distant sound of sirens could be heard, but whether they were from ambulances or squad cars, no one remembers.

"But he was already dead."

CPSIA information can be obtained
at www.ICGtesting.com
Printed in the USA
LVHW090431300721
694057LV00011B/1943